The Blessing Bell

Lynell Hecht

Copyright © 2016 by Lynell Hecht

All rights reserved. No part of this book may be reproduced, stored in a retrieval system, or transmitted by any means without the written permission of the author.

Printed in the United States of America

Written by Lynell Hecht

Illustrations by Casey Smith

Graphic Design by Mike Bullard

First Printing, 2016

Version 1.0

ISBN 978-0-9973046-1-9

The Blessing Bell Company

Memphis, TN

www.theblessingbell.com

Dedication

This book is dedicated to my mother, Carla, who is the inspiration behind *The Blessing Bell*.

It is also dedicated to my husband, Paul, and sons, Samuel and Grady, who bring many blessings and joy to my life.

The Blessing Bell

The sound of the bells rang beautifully in the air. Another child had been welcomed into their small village. That was two times this week!

For several years, Paul and Sarah had hoped to hear the bells ring out for them. They had finally gotten their wish. Soon, they were to welcome a child of their own. This child would be a blessing, and that is what they planned to name their baby. Blessing.

Paul had been working for weeks on a special gift. Each night, it wasn't quite right, but tonight was different. It was the right size. It was very smooth and elegantly shaped. The sound was pure. He polished it to a bright shine. It was perfect. Paul had made the most beautiful bell for Blessing. The village bells would ring, but this bell was going to be especially for Blessing.

The very next day, Blessing was born. Paul and Sarah thought she was perfect, just like the bell. Paul rang it loudly, along with the village bells.

This bell would always be called **The Blessing Bell**.

The Blessing Bell rang when Blessing took her first steps. It rang for each holiday and each birthday. The bell rang jubilantly when Blessing lost her first tooth! There were so many special moments to celebrate.

It was always kept safely next to her bed. When Blessing had a nightmare and was too afraid to cry out, she could ring the bell. Although it did not happen often, her papa quickly came to reassure her that everything was okay.

It rang when she learned to ride her bike. Her first dance, her wedding, and the birth of her own children were all occasions to hear its beautiful sound.

The Blessing Bell rang many times over the years. Traditions were created along the way with her children and grandchildren. It was always close by for celebrations, milestones, and even in times of sickness.

Old and young had heard the special sound. Years had passed, and like its people, the bell grew old. The maker of the bell was no longer there to answer its ring, and others had taken over this job.

The bell showed signs of aging. The handle was worn, and its once brilliant metal had grown dull. The sound, though, was unchanged. It still had that same pure tone that it had the night Blessing's father so carefully crafted it. It was perhaps even more beautiful, for now it provided memories from times gone by.

Blessing was now an old woman. Over the last few years, she had become sick more and more frequently. When Blessing's voice had been too weak to be heard, the bell had been her voice.

Another generation was soon to be born and Blessing knew that it was time for the bell to be passed down. At the child's birth, the crystal clear tone of the bell resonated through the air.

This would be the last time that Blessing heard the sound of the bell her father had made so many years ago. So many memories had been made. There would be so many more to come.

The bell now belonged to a beautiful little girl, whose name was very special.

Her name was Blessing.

The Blessing Bell

Ring this bell when you receive it,
And always keep it near.
Ring it for celebrations
To add to joy and cheer.
Ring it when you are afraid or sick
And when your voice may not be heard.
Help is just a ring away
Your need can be answered.
Ring this bell for rites of passage
For good times and the bad
Some occasions will be happy
And some moments will be sad.
Pass this bell on to a loved one
With stories you can tell
Of memories in your life
That include The Blessing Bell.

About the Author

An educator for over 20 years, Lynell lives in Memphis, TN with her husband and two sons. She loves to share and hear stories of family traditions that have been passed on for generations.

The Author's Bell Tradition

As a child, my family had a special bell in our house that we rang on many occasions. From celebrations, to having it by a bedside in case of a nightmare or when one of us had a stomach bug, this bell was put to good use. There were four children in our family and we often joked about which one of us would inherit this highly coveted bell. That was no longer a question when it was lost in a house fire. As adults, we all found bells of our own. And the traditions continued.

— Lynell Hecht

Traditions and Memories with Special Bells...

Some of my earliest and fondest memories include the ringing of bells. It started at my grandparents' house. When I was a young girl, my family and I loved spending time at their home. We lived in the same town, so visits to their home were frequent and fun. Our visits were never complete until we rolled down our windows so that we could hear them ring the 'Comeback Bell' as we drove away. My grandparents would stand on their back porch steps and ring the bell as we waved to them from the station wagon. We could hear them ring the bell well into the next block. As years went by, I moved from my home in Florida to attend college in Tennessee. Visits home always concluded with the Comeback Bell. As I drove my own car out of their driveway, I would roll my window down, and drive as slowly as I could so I could hear the bell for as long as possible. When my husband and I married, my mother gave everyone a small bell to ring instead of throwing rice. Of course, the windows were rolled down as we drove away to the sound of our family and friends ringing the bells. Twenty-two years and three sons later, we continue to ring our Comeback Bell for family and friends upon their departure from our home. Although my grandparents are no longer on this earth, their bell has a special place at our front door and it serves as a steadfast reminder of their warmth, their love, and the comfort of coming home.

— Mary Call Proctor Ford

> We have a bell in our family that we take turns using for special requests. Admittedly, I use it the most, but my daughter is still in the 'pleaser' stage. Each Saturday morning, I ring the bell. Soon to follow is the most beautiful pink-cheeked little girl with a cup of coffee in my favorite mug. What better way to start off my day? A dose of caffeine and a snuggle from the giggling 'coffee lady!'
> — Val Kemme-Smith

> My husband and I have always enjoyed travel. We began to collect bells from around the world for our only granddaughter, Lucy. One of her favorite bells came from trips her grandfather made to Korea as a Major General in the U.S. Army. These Buddhist Temple Bells are shaped differently from most bells. They have an elongated design and do not gain sound by a clapper inside the bell. Korean bells have a spot on the outer body of the bell called the 'dangjwa' that is struck with a swinging wooden log in order to make its mysterious sound. The dangjwa usually consists of a beautiful design depicting a fairy rising to heaven. Legend has it that because of this uniquely shaped bell, the sound continues to reverberate forever.
> — Major General Retired and Mrs. Paul F. Hamm

> We have a bell that gets passed from person to person in our immediate family. When one of us has a special day, such as a birthday, Mother's Day, or Father's Day, the appropriate individual gains possession the night before. Beginning the

next morning, the bell may be rung for coffee or breakfast in bed, a snack, a shoulder massage, or a chore. Reminders have to sometimes be given not to take advantage of this privilege, as there is always a person that will have it after they do!

— Kimberly Russoniello

Since I was a young child, each time we go on a trip, we have always collected Christmas ornaments for our tree. Our favorite Christmas movie is *It's a Wonderful Life*, and at the end, the little girl says, 'Every time a bell rings, an angel gets its wings.' My mother, grandmother (her mom), and I began the tradition of collecting bells on these trips as well. My father passed away when I was little, so his mother, whom I infrequently got to see, got me a bell each year...sort of a way to remember my dad and his side of the family. Our tradition with these bells is so meaningful, and it touches both sides of my family. We have enough to go around the tree several times. Of course, we start them at the bottom because that part jingles the most. These bells tell one long story as you go around the tree and make each Christmas even more special.

— Brooke Haley

Growing up on 6 1/2 acres on the riverfront in Florida, we spent our summers in and by the water. We hated to go inside because we were always having too much fun chasing fiddler crabs or taking a leaky rowboat equipped with Maxwell House coffee cans. While one would bail, the others would row to an island and we hunted for 'treasures'. If the mosquitoes didn't chase us indoors before supper, my mother would ring a large bell attached to a rope (It was really a fire alarm bell). We could hear that bell instantly, whereas we couldn't hear our mother shouting for us to come home. To this day, I still have a penchant for bells and have collected quite a few. My favorite bell is one we purchased at an antique store. It's a large brass bell attached to a huge leather belt that was formally worn by a cow in Germany."

— Carla P. Smith

"My sister and I grew up next to a school park, and in the summertime there was always something going on. It was understood that we weren't allowed inside the house just to loaf around and watch television, so naturally we would wander over to the park. Whenever my mother needed us, she would ring a big black bell that was affixed to the wall off of our back door. Not only did we look forward to hearing it, as we knew it meant a reprieve from the heat, but our friends in the neighborhood would also use it as their cue to head home in the hopes they might also be allowed into the air-conditioning for an hour or so. We still tease my mother today about making us suffer out in the summer heat, but we both still remember the sound of that bell ringing and the joy it brought us to be welcomed home."

— Michael Driscoll

Traditions and Memories From Our Family...

CPSIA information can be obtained
at www.ICGtesting.com
Printed in the USA
LVHW042119190723
752798LV00004B/170